Treasure Hunt

By

Heidi Martin

Treasure Hunt, Published December, 2013

Interior and Cover Illustrations: Lisa Marie Brennan
Interior Layout: Howard Johnson, Howard Communigrafix, Inc.
Editorial: Eden Rivers Editorial Services
Proofreading: Susan Herbert and Karen Grennan

 SDP Publishing

Published by SDP Publishing an imprint of SDP Publishing Solutions, LLC.

For more information about this book contact Lisa Akoury-Ross by email at
lross@SDPPublising.com.

Library of Congress Control Number: 2013953078

ISBN-13 (print): 978-0-9889381-8-2
ISBN-13 (ebook): 978-0-9899723-4-5

Printed in the United States of America

Acknowledgments

I would like to thank my husband, Matthew, for all of his love and support during this entire process. You encouraged me and sacrificed so much for this dream of mine to become a reality. Also, I want to thank my children, Adeline and Malachi. It is your treasure hunts and love of exploring that inspired me to create this book. The two of you are a bright light for me each day. May you always have that unbridled enthusiasm for life.

Thank you to my parents, Paul and Phyllis, who have been through so much this past year. You both are an inspiration each and every day. Thanks for always believing in me.

Thank you to my aunts, two excellent educators, Barb and Sue, for their input and ideas. Your insights helped make this book the best that it could be. And I can't forget my uncle, Dan, whose creative treasure hunts are always fun for the whole family!

Thank you to my editors, Lisa Schleipfer and Susan Herbert, for their revisions and ideas that brought this book to fruition. Your senses of humor and encouragement along the way were very much appreciated. Also, thank you to Lisa Akoury-Ross, my publisher, for all of her guidance and support during this entire process. Your advice meant more than you can imagine!

Finally, thank you to my illustrator, Lisa Brennan. You are an amazing artist whose pictures have really brought this book to life. You've created something beautiful. Thank you!

To my children, Adeline and Malachi. May you always have the courage to follow your dreams.

Treasure hunt, treasure hunt, on our way,
We will make it back some day.

First to the garden pumpkin patch,
See the gate, unlock the latch.
Treasure hunt, treasure hunt, on our way,
What will we discover today?

Next to trees with trunks so large,
Sticks to play with, who's in charge?
Treasure hunt, treasure hunt, on our way,
In these woods we will not stay.

Off to the stream, mud near the edge,
Stomp right over to the ledge.
Treasure hunt, treasure hunt, on our way,
Is the river bottom made of clay?

Tromp through the water flowing fast,
Will the treasure rush right past?
Treasure hunt, treasure hunt, on our way,
Can you feel the river's spray?

Sopping wet, we reach the plain,
With flowers, insects, and a crane.
Treasure hunt, treasure hunt, on our way,
See the grasses start to sway.

Here at the mountain, should we go?
Up to the top from here below?
Treasure hunt, treasure hunt, on our way,
Keep on going, do not stray.

We climb to the peak, way up high,
The wind sounds like a baby's cry.
Treasure hunt, treasure hunt, on our way,
The slippery rocks are large and gray.

There in the bushes crouching low,
With big, yellow eyes all aglow.
Treasure hunt, treasure hunt, on our way,
Is it something we have to slay?

It jumps right out, giving us a scare,
At least it's not a big, black bear.
Treasure hunt, treasure hunt, on our way,
Hearts still pounding, we're okay.

We wander down a rocky road,
To a cave that's damp and cold.
Treasure hunt, treasure hunt, on our way,
Is it safe? Should we walk away?

We hold our breath and tiptoe in,
With lights in hand, we start to grin.
Treasure hunt, treasure hunt, on our way,
We have found them, hip hip hooray.

Sleeping at the cave's great height,
Bodies of black are quite the sight.
Treasure hunt, treasure hunt, on our way,
We must watch this grand display.

We take the picture in a flash,
And leave that cave so very fast.
Treasure hunt, treasure hunt, on our way,
Keep to the path, do not delay!

Are they chasing us? We do not know,
We run like lightning to the fields below.
Treasure hunt, treasure hunt, on our way,
Across the meadow, through the hay.

Into the river and amongst the trees,
And through the garden with a sneeze.
Treasure hunt, treasure hunt, on our way,
We're back at the schoolhouse by midday.

What was the treasure way up there?
Can you take a guess? Will you share?
Treasure hunt, treasure hunt, on our way,
They're fuzzy and small, wouldn't you say?

Bats of course, black bats they are,
With wings that take them oh so far.
Treasure hunt, treasure hunt, on our way,
We learned something new, what a day!

The animals we found are all unique,
They grunt and caw and sometimes squeak.
Treasure hunt, treasure hunt, on our way,
Now it's time for us to play!

TREASURES FOR TODAY

Our teacher hands us a surprise,
An animal pencil and a fun disguise.
Treasure hunt, treasure hunt, oh what fun!
What a treasure we have won!

About the Author

A Minnesota native, Heidi Martin spends her days as an educator, tutoring students in reading, writing, and math. She began writing as a hobby, and was inspired to create a children's book by her own two children when they began exploring in their yard one sunny afternoon. Watching their excitement, Heidi scratched down a story about a treasure hunt, which she read to them. They enjoyed it so much that she decided to make it into a book. Heidi lives in Massachusetts with her husband and children.

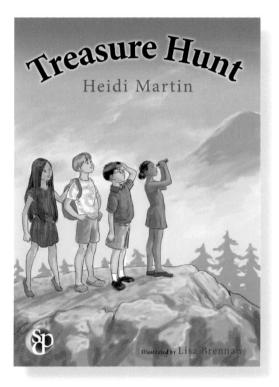

Treasure Hunt

Heidi Martin

Children's book, ages 4-8

Website: heidimartinbooks.com

Facebook: facebook.com/heidimartinbooks

Publisher: SDP Publishing

Also available in ebook format

TO PURCHASE:

Amazon.com

BarnesAndNoble.com

SDPPublishingSolutions.com

www.SDPPublishingSolutions.com

Contact us at: info@SDPPublishing.com

CPSIA information can be obtained
at www.ICGtesting.com
Printed in the USA
BVIC01n1146090114
341213BV00002B/3

* 9 7 8 0 9 8 8 9 3 8 1 8 2 *